Best Wishes

[signature]

THE ADVENTURES OF CHUGGALUG

James McClelland

MINERVA PRESS
ATLANTA LONDON SYDNEY

THE ADVENTURES OF CHUGGALUG
Copyright © James McClelland 1999

ISBN 0 75410 555 5

First Published 1999 by
MINERVA PRESS
315–317 Regent Street
London W1R 7YB

Printed in Great Britain for Minerva Press

THE ADVENTURES OF CHUGGALUG

Chuggalug Makes a Friend

Once upon a time, in the days when dinosaurs roamed the earth, a little boy called Chuggalug lived with his mummy and daddy in a lovely big tree house. Chuggalug's daddy had built the tree house high in the branches of a magnificent oak tree, in a clearing deep in the deepest part of the great Caledonian forest, in a place called Abernethy.

Chuggalug loved his tree house. It was built of logs and had a veranda right round the outside. From his bedroom window Chuggalug could look out across the tops of the forest trees, and watch the birds soaring above the forest looking for food. At the edge of the clearing, the water of the River Nethy sparkled in the sunshine, and gurgled over the rocks on its way to the great loch far away. In the distance he could see the dark shape of the great mountains of Cairngorm.

One day he saw a huge flying dinosaur called a pteranodon flying low over the trees. Chuggalug leaned out of his window, fascinated by the enormous wings and the enormous beak of the pteranodon.

The pteranodon spotted Chuggalug at the window. 'Aha,' he said, 'that looks like a very tasty little boy, I think I'll have him for tea.'

The pteranodon swooped down, straight towards Chuggalug, who stared and stared as the great beast came closer and closer. 'Ha ha ha, hee hee hee, tonight I'll have a little boy for tea,' he screeched.

Closer and closer came the monster with his great beak wide open. He was just about to snatch Chuggalug from the window, when the chair he was standing on suddenly fell backwards, and Chuggalug fell into his bedroom, bounced on his bed, and landed right under the table in the corner.

The pteranodon soared up into the sky, furious at missing the little boy, and went off in search of some other titbit for his tea.

Chuggalug got up from the floor and went through to the kitchen where his mummy was baking some cakes.

Now Chuggalug was a good boy and listened when his mummy and daddy told him that the forest was dangerous, and that he was not to wander off from the tree house alone. Sometimes, however, when he was playing a very good game, or having an exciting adventure, he would forget to be good, and wandered off alone.

One day Chuggalug was playing at being a hunter, and was searching around the clearing for a good stick to make into a spear.

He searched farther and farther from the tree house, and deeper and deeper into the forest. He was so busy looking up at the trees and bushes for a good stick that he suddenly found himself falling through space.

With a crash he landed at the bottom of a deep hole in a bed of leaves, The hole was dark and damp, and had steep slippery sides, so try and try as he might, Chuggalug couldn't climb out.

He became frightened and wished that he had remembered his mummy and daddy's warnings about not wandering into the forest alone.

He sat down on the leaves to think about what he could do.

Then Chuggalug heard a noise. A deep groany growly sound came from the other end of the hole. He peered into the darkness. The biggest, yellowest pair of eyes he had ever seen were staring at him from the other side of the dark hole.

Chuggalug was very frightened. He screwed up his eyes to see better, and there, in the hole with him, was a huge sabre-toothed tiger.

The tiger and the boy stared at each other for ages. Why doesn't it eat me? thought Chuggalug.

He saw the two great sabre teeth hanging from the mouth of the great beast and knew that it could eat him any time it wanted.

Once again the tiger made a soft groany growly noise. Chuggalug was still staring at the big yellow eyes when he noticed a great big tear falling from the corner of one of them.

Chuggalug looked closely at the tiger, not so frightened now, and saw that the beast was holding up one of its big furry paws. Underneath the paw, in the soft part behind the row of enormous razor-sharp claws, Chuggalug saw a large thorn sticking out.

Chuggalug could see that the sabre-toothed tiger was in pain and needed help. He crept forward towards the huge injured beast, whose head was the same size as Chuggalug, and gently reached out and pulled out the thorn from the tiger's paw.

The sabre-toothed tiger gave a soft, deep purr of pleasure. It stood up and came towards Chuggalug, who started to get frightened again as it came closer and closer.

It was right next to him. Chuggalug closed his eyes and thought, This is it. This is when I get eaten.

Then he felt a huge, warm, wet, soft thing slide up his face. It was the tiger's huge, warm, wet soft tongue licking his face. Chuggalug giggled, for the tongue was tickly. He then put his arms round the tiger's great neck and gave it a great big hug.

When the sabre-toothed tiger stood up, it was huge! Chuggalug could see that its shoulder was level with the top of the hole. The sabre-toothed tiger lay down again, and Chuggalug sat on its great, broad furry back.

When the tiger stood up, Chuggalug easily climbed out of the hole onto the grass.

With one bound, the sabre-toothed tiger jumped out of the hole and stood beside Chuggalug. Chuggalug looked round and realised two things all at once. It was getting dark, and he didn't know how to get hone.

The big furry sabre-toothed tiger looked at Chuggalug and seemed to understand. Again the tiger lay down and Chuggalug climbed on its back.

The tiger set off through the forest with Chuggalug, travelling along in great leaps and bounds. Chuggalug rode along, holding on to the thick fur of its neck, laughing and shouting, 'Boing boing, boing boing,' in time with the tiger's steps.

'I know.' said Chuggalug, 'You can be my friend. I'll call you Boing Boing.'

Chuggalug's mummy and daddy were getting worried, and were just about to set out to look for him, when they heard the thump thump thump of a large animal running towards the tree house.

Chuggalug's daddy raised his spear, ready to fight whatever it was that was running towards them. His eyes opened wide with amazement when he saw, running from the jungle, an enormous, fierce looking sabre-toothed tiger, with Chuggalug sitting on its back, laughing and shouting.

'Daddy, Daddy,' called Chuggalug 'This is my new friend. He's called Boing Boing. He got me out of a big hole. I pulled a thorn from his paw. He brought me home. Can I keep him for my pet? Can I? Can I? Please, please, please, can I?'

'Just a moment, just a moment,' laughed Chuggalug's daddy. 'Sabre-toothed tigers are not pets. They are very fierce and dangerous animals, so I don't think that Boing Boing can ever be your pet.'

Chuggalug started to feel very sad, but then heard his daddy say, 'however, there's nothing to stop him being your friend. He will be free to wander the forest as he wants, and you can still be friends.'

Chuggalug was a very happy and tired little boy when he went to bed that night, high up in his room in the tree house. Just before he drifted off to sleep he heard a loud roar from the forest. But he wasn't frightened. He knew it was a friendly roar. He knew it was Boing Boing, the best friend a boy ever had, and he just knew that they would have many adventures together.

Chuggalug and the
Loch Ness Monster

Chuggalug was bored. It was the rainy season in the forest and he had been stuck indoors for ages and ages, while outdoors the rain seemed to have been pouring down for ever and ever.

He was sitting at the window of his bedroom in the tree house, gazing out across the forest, dreaming of the wonderful adventures he could have with his friend Boing Boing the sabre-toothed tiger. If only the rain would stop!

Then, suddenly, Chuggalug saw a shaft of sunlight come down through the clouds and the rain stopped. The leaves of the trees, and the grass in the clearing round the great oak tree which held the tree house, started glistening in the sunshine.

He looked up and saw the patch of blue sky spreading and spreading until the huge yellow sun was shining all over the forest.

He heard the forest come to life again. The birds started chirping and whistling, and it seemed the whole world was happy that the rain had stopped.

Then Chuggalug heard a loud roar from the forest.

'It's Boing Boing!' he shouted, and jumped down from the window. He ran through the house and out on to the veranda. He quickly climbed down the long rope ladder which hung down to the ground, and ran off excitedly across the clearing beneath the tree house and into the forest.

Now Chuggalug had often been told by his mummy and daddy that the forest was dangerous, and that he should never go off alone. But he was so happy that the rain had stopped and that he was going to meet Boing Boing, that he completely forgot, and anyway, it was such a lovely sunny day after all the rain, that nothing bad could possibly happen.

Chuggalug ran and ran and ran, shouting for Boing Boing. Every time he heard another roar from the forest, he ran faster and faster.

Suddenly Chuggalug found himself falling through the air. He had been running so fast that he didn't see where the path had been washed away by the rain.

He fell and fell, over and over, and landed with a bump. But he didn't stop. He slithered and slipped down a steep slope. He slid faster and faster down the muddy slope, rushing round corners and down and down until, with a mighty splash, he plunged into the river, fast flowing and deep, with the flood waters swirling all around.

Chuggalug was swept along helplessly. The rushing, roaring water, whirled him round and round and over and over until he didn't know which way was which.

Chuggalug was very scared. He was gasping for breath. The water was over his head. He struggled to reach the surface to get some air, just when he thought

he would never breathe again, he felt a bump and caught hold of an old gnarled tree trunk, which was floating down the river.

Chuggalug pulled himself up on to the tree trunk and lay on his tummy among the branches, holding on tightly in case he fell into the water again. The river carried him on and on, further and further downstream, and further and further away from the tree house and his mummy and daddy.

On and on he drifted, sometimes sleeping and sometimes awake, wondering if he would ever see his mummy and daddy again.

Then Chuggalug noticed that the banks of the river were getting further and further away. The river was getting wider and wider, until he saw that he was no longer drifting down a river, but was floating out into a huge loch.

Chuggalug sat up on the tree trunk and looked all round. The dark waters of the loch were surrounded on both sides by dark, steeply sloping mountains.

Suddenly Chuggalug remembered his daddy telling him about a great loch whose dark waters were surrounded by steep mountains. It was called Loch Ness and was a dangerous place.

He tried to paddle the tree trunk back towards the side of the loch, desperately paddling with his hands and his feet, but the tree trunk was too heavy. Very slowly he drifted towards the middle of the loch. The banks of the loch looked smaller and smaller until everywhere he looked, Chuggalug could see nothing but water all around him.

It was very quiet, only the sound of the water lapping against the tree trunk disturbing the silence. Chuggalug shouted for help, but he knew that he was so far away from land that no one could possibly hear him.

Chuggalug was lying on his tummy, slowly paddling with his hands, his face near the water. Suddenly there was a disturbance on the surface, close to his face, and there, right in front of him, was the biggest head Chuggalug had ever seen.

It was a huge scaly head with two big green eyes, and they looked at him curiously. But more frightening was the mouth. The beast's head was massive, and he knew that he could easily be swallowed up by that huge mouth.

Chuggalug tried not to scream. He didn't want to startle the monster, which was still watching him closely.

It was very difficult not to scream when the head started to rise out of the water on a very long neck. At the same time another head appeared beside Chuggalug, just as big as the first one, and started to sniff him.

Chuggalug sat up an the tree trunk to look at the monsters. Both beasts immediately disappeared beneath the water. Then to Chuggalug's surprise a third head appeared beside him.

This one didn't frighten Chuggalug. It was much smaller than the other two and was obviously a baby monster.

'Hello,' said the little monster, 'what are you?'

'I'm a boy,' said Chuggalug, 'and I'm lost. Who are you and who are those other two big monsters? Please ask them not to eat me.'

'I'm a plesiosaur,' said the small beast, 'and that's my mummy and daddy. We live in the loch. We won't eat you. I'll get my daddy. He'll help you.'

Then the two large plesiosaurs reappeared, their huge heads rising out of the water on their long necks, high above Chuggalug.

'Hello little boy,' said the daddy plesiosaur, 'how did you get yourself into this fix? I bet your mummy and daddy don't know where you are.'

'No, they don't,' said Chuggalug, 'and if I'd done what my mummy and daddy told me and not run off into the forest alone, I wouldn't be here.'

'Exactly,' said the mummy plesiosaur. 'Little boys, and little plesiosaurs, should always listen to their mummy and daddy. It would keep them out of trouble.'

'Now then,' said daddy plesiosaur, 'how can we help you? We can only push you to the shore, but you'll have to get home through the forest by yourself. Do you know how to get home?'

'No,' said Chuggalug, 'I don't.' He was feeling very sorry for himself and felt very silly for not doing as his mummy and daddy had told him.

'Well, let's get you to the side of the loch and on to dry land first,' said daddy plesiosaur. He pushed the tree trunk with Chuggalug sitting on it towards the shore of the loch.

The had almost reached the edge of the loch, with mummy and baby plesiosaur swimming alongside,

when they heard a huge roar from the forest at the side of the loch.

'Oh dear,' said mummy plesiosaur. 'How ever will you get home through the forest with all the wild animals running about? Whatever can we do?'

'Don't worry,' said Chuggalug, laughing. 'I can see the wild animal. It's my friend Boing Boing, the sabre-toothed tiger. I'll be all right now. He'll take me home safely.'

When the tree trunk reached the edge of the loch, Chuggalug jumped on to the beach. Boing Boing ran towards him.

'Come on Chuggalug,' said Boing Boing. 'Jump on my back and let's get you home before it gets dark. I followed you down the river when you fell in, but I couldn't follow you out into the loch.

Chuggalug climbed on to Boing Boing's back. He looked round and saw the three long necks sticking out of the water as the plesiosaurs watched him anxiously.

'Goodbye,' he shouted. 'Thank you all for helping me.'

'Goodbye,' called the plesiosaurs. 'And remember,' said mummy plesiosaurus, 'you must do what your mummy tells you in future, and stay out of trouble.'

'I will,' said Chuggalug. 'Goodbye.'

Boing Boing soon had Chuggalug back home, and watched him as he ran across the clearing and climbed up the rope ladder back safely into the tree house.

Chuggalug ran through to his bedroom and over to the window to watch Boing Boing disappear into the forest.

He was still sitting at the window when his mummy called to him. 'Chuggalug, the rain has been stopped for a while, if you want to go out to play.'

'No thank you,' said Chuggalug, who thought he'd had enough adventure for one day.

Chuggalug and Pteranodon

Chuggalug was playing with his cart. It was a wooden cart, with four wooden wheels, which his daddy had made for him. Chuggalug thought it was the best cart in the world and loved pulling it along by the vine rope attached to the front.

He was lying back in the cart with his arms hanging over the sides, half dozing in the warm sunshine, remembering the days he spent, by his daddy's side, watching him building it. He had watched him shape the wheels, and now remembered that lovely feeling he'd felt, knowing that his daddy was building it especially for him. Chuggalug always enjoyed remembering that feeling.

As he sat there, his gaze wandered around the clearing under the giant oak tree which was the tallest in the forest, and which held the tree house in its topmost branches. His slowly wandering eyes rested on a huge sabre-toothed tiger which was sleeping at the edge of the clearing, purring deeply as it slept. It was not easy to spot, its striped coat mingling with the dappled yellow sunlight which fell on the grass through the gently rustling leaves of the forest trees.

Chuggalug was not afraid of the huge tiger. The tiger was Chuggalug's very best friend. His name was Boing Boing and he and Chuggalug had had many adventures together in the forest.

Lying lazily in his cart, Chuggalug had an idea. It would be fun to play a trick on Boing Boing and give him a fright. He remembered that his mummy and daddy had often told him never never never to startle a sleeping animal whether it was a dog, a cat or anything, but, as boys and girls often do, he thought that 'just this once' it would be fun.

He climbed out of his cart and, pulling it along behind him, he crept quietly across the clearing to where Boing Boing was sleeping. As he got nearer he could hear the deep purring of the huge beast as it slept. Chuggalug smiled to himself as he thought of the trick he was going to play. Although he didn't really feel he was being naughty or bad, he still glanced back towards the oak tree and the tree house to make sure his mummy and daddy were not watching.

He tiptoed up to Boing Boing and, as quietly as a mouse, tied the vine rope to the tiger's tail. He then crept back to the cart and climbed in. Trying not to laugh, Chuggalug picked up a stick from the ground and, with a loud shout which shattered the silence in the clearing, he threw the stick, hitting Boing Boing on the head. As all boys and girls know, there is a time when you are being naughty when you suddenly wish you hadn't, and this was the time for Chuggalug.

When the stick hit him on the head Boing Boing leapt up and, hearing the loud noise behind him, ran off without looking round, away from whatever danger was behind him. He was confused and realised that something had a grip of his tail and was running after him just as fast as he was. This made him run faster and faster, farther and farther into the forest. Boing Boing was running blindly, just trying to outrun the thing behind him, and had no idea where he was running to.

Chuggalug had fallen backwards into the cart when Boing Boing started to run, and was now being tossed about, this way and that, upside down and round about. He was yelling and shouting for Boing Boing to stop but the noise of the cart's wooden wheels rattling and crashing on the stones was so loud that the great tiger couldn't hear his yells. Boing Boing was roaring like thunder and all the little animals were scattering out of the way as the huge tiger crashed through the forest, the wooden cart with Chuggalug in it clattering along behind it.

Then it happened. Suddenly the forest cleared and Boing Boing found himself at the edge of a huge cliff. He turned quickly and ran back towards the trees.

The cart hit a large boulder at the cliff edge and smashed into a thousand pieces. Chuggalug was thrown up into the air and straight over the edge of the cliff.

Chuggalug found himself falling, tumbling over and over and over, towards the jagged rocks far far below. He was screaming and shouting, but he knew no one could hear him. The rocks came closer and closer and Chuggalug closed his eyes. He felt the wind blowing against his face and tugging at his hair as he fell faster and faster towards the rocks.

Then something strange happened. Chuggalug suddenly felt himself stop falling. He seemed to be flying up into the sky. He opened his eyes and saw that he had not hit the rocks, but was soaring high above them, getting higher and higher. He could see the cliffs and the forest trees getting smaller and smaller below him.

Chuggalug started to laugh and laugh, and then he saw why he was flying so high, why he had not crashed into the rocks, and he stopped laughing. An enormous pteranodon had him in its massive beak, and was carrying him high into the sky. He looked around to see where it was heading for and his heart sank. Ahead he could see the pteranodon's nest high up on a ledge near the top of a mountain.

'Oh dear,' thought Chuggalug. 'I'm for it now. The pteranodon is taking me to its nest to eat me. If only Boing Boing was here to save me.' He felt very scared and wished he hadn't played such a cruel trick on his best friend.

The pteranodon flew on towards its nest carrying poor Chuggalug in its beak. As it landed on the ledge near the top of the mountain, it dropped Chuggalug into the bottom of the huge nest. Chuggalug had his eyes closed again and tumbled into the nest. Then he heard lots of squawking and squealing, and opening his eyes saw that he was sitting in the bottom of the nest, surrounded by four baby pteranodons.

'Mummy, mummy what is that thing?' cried one of the babies, poking curiously at Chuggalug with its beak.

'Hey! That tickles,' shouted Chuggalug, falling backwards into the bottom of the nest, laughing. The baby pteranodons, seeing Chuggalug laughing, all started to cackle and laugh too.

'It's a baby human,' said the mummy pteranodon, trying to keep her voice stern amidst all the laughter. 'And I think he's in trouble. If I hadn't spotted him falling over the cliff and caught him, I don't know what would have happened.' The baby pteranodons stopped laughing and looked at Chuggalug curiously.

'Can't you fly?' said one.

'Where's your wings?' said another.

'How do you eat with no beak?' said a third.

'How did you fall over the cliff?' asked the fourth.

Chuggalug took a deep breath and told them the whole story, from tying the rope to Boing Boing's tail, to landing in the bottom of their nest. At the end of the story he was feeling very sorry for himself and was struggling not to cry.

'Well!' said the mummy pteranodon. 'I hope your friend, the tiger, is all right after the fright you gave him. I don't suppose he expected his best friend to do such a thing, do you?' she said, looking sternly at Chuggalug.

'Nnno,' he stammered. 'I don't think he would. Do you think he'll still be my friend?'

'I really don't know,' said the mummy pteranodon. 'But I think I'd better try to get you home before it gets dark.'

Chuggalug couldn't tell the mummy pteranodon how to get home to the tree house in the forest where he lived. He had bounced about in the cart for so long behind Boing Boing that he had no idea which direction they had come or how far they had travelled.

'I'll just have to take you back to the cliff where I found you,' said the mummy pteranodon. 'Perhaps you'll remember from there.'

Chuggalug said goodbye to the baby pteranodons, who said they'd try to find his tree house and visit him once they learned how to fly. The mummy pteranodon picked him up in her enormous beak and soared over the forest back towards the cliff.

Chuggalug scanned the treetops below looking for familiar signs which might guide him home, but everything was strange and he began to think he would never get home again.

Then, as they flew over the top of the cliff, Chuggalug heard a loud roar. 'Listen!' he shouted. 'That's Boing Boing!' He looked down and there at the edge of the forest, near the cliff was a huge sabre-toothed tiger looking up at them.

'Okay,' said the mummy pteranodon. 'I'll fly low over him and drop you beside him, and I hope you remember to say you're sorry for the way you treated him.'

'I will, and thank you for saving me,' shouted Chuggalug.

The great pteranodon swooped low over the clifftop, gently dropped Chuggalug on the grass next to Boing Boing, and soared away, high into the blue sky.

'Goodbye, and thank you,' he shouted, waving his hand. He then turned round slowly and looked at Boing Boing, who was quietly looking down at him.

Chuggalug ran to the giant beast and threw his arms round its front leg, hugged it tight.

'I'm sorry Boing Boing. I've been really bad. Will you still be my friend, please? I'll never do anything bad to you again.'

The great tiger looked at Chuggalug. Then Boing Boing bent down and licked his face with its enormous soft wet tongue. Chuggalug was so happy he just laughed and laughed, Boing Boing lay down on the ground to let Chuggalug climb on to his back and then they bounded off through the forest back to the clearing with the great oak tree which held the tree house where Chuggalug lived with his mummy and daddy.

Chuggalug climbed down from the tiger's back at the edge of the clearing and, waving goodbye to Boing Boing, ran towards the rope ladder and climbed up to the house.

'Is that you Chuggalug?' called his mummy. 'What have you been up to today?'

'Oh, just playing with Boing Boing,' said Chuggalug as he washed his hands, ready for supper.

Chuggalug meets Tyrannosaurus

Chuggalug was looking for Boing Boing. They were playing at hide-and-seek. Boing Boing was very difficult to find in the forest. He was a huge sabre-toothed tiger and was Chuggalug's best friend. His yellow and black stripes made him very hard to see when he lay hiding in the bushes in the dappled sunshine.

Chuggalug crept through the forest as quietly as he could, listening for the slightest sound to give him a clue to where Boing Boing was hiding. He would creep forward for a time, then stop and stand perfectly still and listen for ages. He heard nothing but the normal forest noises: the soft wind rustling the leaves on the trees, and the whistles and screeches of small animals far off through the forest – but no Boing Boing!

Boing Boing is too good at this game, thought Chuggalug as he stood listening in a clearing, I wish I could find him, then it will be my turn to hide, and I'll make sure he doesn't find me for ages. Then he heard it. He cocked his ear up and listened very carefully.

Yes, there it was again, a soft purring sound. It was coming from a clump of bushes just in front of him, so Chuggalug sneaked forward, parted the bushes and peered in. There, in the centre of the clump, lay Boing Boing, his huge head resting on his front paws, fast asleep.

With a shout, Chuggalug plunged into the bushes and dived on Boing Boing's back, threw his arms round the great furry neck and yelled.

'I've found you, I've found you. Now it's my turn to go and hide.' Boing Boing got up and with a great roar, stretched himself, the way sabre-toothed tigers do. He then sat up and closed his eyes so that Chuggalug could run off and hide.

Chuggalug ran and ran as fast as his legs would carry him, farther and farther into the deepest and darkest part of the forest. He was so determined that Boing Boing would not find him that he had no idea bow far he was running, or where he was running to.

Eventually Chuggalug found a thick clump of bushes, at the edge of a clearing in the forest, which looked perfect to hide in. He looked round about, and realised that he was in a strange part of the forest, a part of the forest which his daddy had often told him to stay away from. He frowned, feeling slightly uneasy for a moment. But then he thought, It'll be all right, just this once, and anyway, Boing Boing will find me soon and it'll be okay.

He pushed his way into the bushes and sat down quietly to wait for Boing Boing to find him.

He listened for Boing Boing coming, but he really knew that he wouldn't hear him because the huge tiger could pad silently through the forest and Chuggalug never ever heard him coming.

Then Chuggalug heard a deep booming sound away in the distance, Boom, boom, boom, boom, far away, but getting closer. 'What can that be?' he wondered aloud. Boom, boom, boom, boom, closer still. 'I know,' he thought nervously, 'It's Boing Boing looking for me, and he's making that noise so I won't think it's him.' He smiled to himself and snuggled deeper into the bushes.

BOOM, BOOM, BOOM, BOOM. It was really close now. Chuggalug could feel the ground shaking underneath him, and was getting a bit frightened. 'I hope it is Boing Boing, I don't know what it can be if it's not.'

BOOM, BOOM, BOOM, BOOM. The ground was really shaking now and Chuggalug knew that it wasn't Boing Boing.

He crawled to the edge of the bushes, slowly parted them with his hands and looked out. For the first time Chuggalug was face to face with tyrannosaurus rex, the biggest, fiercest dinosaur of them all.

Chuggalug watched fixed to the spot, as the gigantic beast looked round the clearing. He stood very still, as his daddy had once told him that most dinosaurs had poor eyesight, and that if you didn't move, they probably wouldn't see you. He also remembered that his daddy had told him to stay out of this part of the forest, and wished that he had done what he was told.

It seemed that his daddy was right, as the huge dinosaur didn't seen to see him and was still standing

up, its head as high as the top branches of the trees, looking round the clearing.

Chuggalug was just starting to feel slightly better, and to think that maybe the tyrannosaurus wouldn't find him after all, when he felt himself start to lose his balance. He had leaned too far forward, and now fell out of the bushes into the clearing. He desperately tried to get his balance, but suddenly tumbled out, with a crash, into the clearing, right in front of tyrannosaurus rex.

The dinosaur turned round quickly, and let out a giant roar. It bent down and looked at Chuggalug as he lay on the grass. It let out another roar, and Chuggalug could smell its horrible breath and see its rows of huge teeth as its great mouth opened above him.

Chuggalug closed his eyes, gulped and tried to shout for help, but he seemed to have lost his voice and couldn't make a sound.

Just as he was sure he was going to be eaten, he heard another great roar from the side of the clearing. This was a different roar, one that Chuggalug knew. He opened his eyes and saw Boing Boing leap, with one mighty bound, high over him and sink his teeth into the giant dinosaur's nose.

'I suppose you think that's funny,' squealed the dinosaur, rubbing its nose with its front feet.

'Yes I do,' laughed Chuggalug, finding his voice again and jumping to his feet. Boing Boing ran round and bit the dinosaur's tail. The huge dinosaur let out another roar and thundered off into the forest, wondering how it could lick its nose and tail at the same time.

Chuggalug laughed and climbed on to Boing Boing's back.

'Let's get home,' he shouted, and the big tiger bounded off through the forest, back to the clearing where Chuggalug lived with his mummy and daddy in a great tree house his daddy had built, high in the branches of a huge oak tree.

Chuggalug jumped down from Boing Boing's back, gave the tiger a big hug, and said, 'You're the best friend a boy could ever have.'

He ran over to the rope ladder which took him up into the tree house. 'Is that you Chuggalug?' his mummy called as she heard him come in. 'Where have you been. Your supper's nearly ready.'

'Oh, I was just outside playing with Boing Boing,' called Chuggalug as he washed his hands. After all his mummy would only worry if he told her about his adventure with Boing Boing and the tyrannosaurus rex.

A Scary Adventure

Chuggalug was very good at climbing trees. He had plenty of trees to practise on, living, as he did, in the great forest which, even from the topmost branches of the tallest trees, stretched in every direction as far as the eye could see.

He had a favourite tree to climb. It was a great oak tree whose branches spread out wider than all the other trees around it. The topmost branch was very strong, and had two small branches just at the right height for Chuggalug to stand on, holding on with one hand, to scan the treetops all round. The branch would sway gently in the breeze, but Chuggalug wasn't scared as he knew it was strong enough to hold him. He loved making the branch swing by leaning one way, then the other, but he always held on tight with one hand.

Chuggalug often wondered what his mummy would say if she saw him swinging high above the ground in the high branches of the great oak tree. He would laugh to himself because he knew that it was his secret tree in his secret part of the forest.

One day Chuggalug was out in the forest looking for his best friend Boing Boing.

Boing Boing was a huge and ferocious looking sabre-toothed tiger, who also lived in the forest. Chuggalug and Boing Boing had been best friends ever since the day when Chuggalug had found the huge tiger in pain, with a large thorn in his foot, and had pulled it out. They had had many adventures together since then and Boing Boing had become Chuggalug's guardian in the forest, keeping him out of trouble when he could, and rescuing him when he couldn't.

After looking and looking for ages and ages, Chuggalug had a good idea. He would go to his favourite oak tree and climb to the top. He could then call to Boing Boing from up there and he would hear him and come running. He ran through the forest, kicking up the piles of golden leaves which had fallen from the trees, until at last he reached the great oak tree.

The bottom branches of the tree looked much too high for Chuggalug to reach, but he found a stick lying on the ground, and, catching the twigs at the end of the bottom branch, pulled the end down until he could jump up and grab the leaves and pull the branch down. He worked his way along the branch towards the tree and, when the branch was thick enough to hold him he caught hold of it with both hands and swung his legs up and over the branch, pulled himself up, and sat on the branch.

Now came the part Chuggalug loved. The branches of the oak tree were all just the right thickness for his foot to stand on or his hand to hold on to, and in no time at all he had reached the top of the tree.

He shaded his eyes from the bright autumn sun with his free hand and looked all round. He felt as if he was at the top of the world, for he could see the forest treetops like a green and gold carpet covering the world, and the bright blue sky, dusted with cotton wool clouds, became the ceiling. Chuggalug felt as if he was the only person in the whole world.

He then started to swing the branch back and for-wards, faster and faster, yelling, 'Boing Booing, Boing Boing,' in time to the swing of the branch. After a few moments Chuggalug heard a loud roar away in the distance and yelled louder still, 'Boing Boing, Boing Boing.'

The roar came again, this time closer, but this time Chuggalug stopped shouting and kept very quiet. That wasn't Boing Boing. It sounded much bigger and not very friendly.

The roar came again, this time very close, and Chuggalug could feel the great oak tree shaking. He looked down, and there, at the bottom of the tree was the biggest, fiercest looking dinosaur Chuggalug had ever seen. It was an allosaurus, one of the biggest and fiercest of them all.

'The enormous beast had heard Chuggalug yelling and was standing up on its hind legs, looking up into the branches of the tree, quietly grunting now and then as if it was talking to itself or thinking about where the noise had come from.

Chuggalug kept perfectly still, for his daddy had once told him that dinosaurs had poor eyesight, and could only see you if you moved. It seemed to be working. The allosaurus slowly walked round the tree,

but obviously could not see or hear Chuggalug, who was being very quiet and very still.

Then he felt the sneeze coming.

As he put his free hand up to his nose, the dinosaur saw the movement and looked up quickly. It all happened at the same time.

The dinosaur let out an enormous roar and shook the oak tree.

Chuggalug could see the huge open mouth below him as he sneezed and lost his grip on the branch. He fell straight down into the gaping mouth of the dinosaur and slid down and down the long tunnel of its throat falling with a bump into the great dark cavern of its tummy.

Chuggalug looked around him. It was completely dark and he could see nothing. He was very frightened and couldn't imagine how he was going to get out.

The dinosaur let out a great roar and as its mouth opened a ray of light showed him the way back up the tunnel he had just come down.

Chuggalug picked up a piece of bone which was lying beside him and began to crawl to the bottom of the tunnel, which was the dinosaur's throat.

The dinosaur continued to roar and roar, which was good because it let Chuggalug see where he was going. It also let him see the rows of huge teeth in the dinosaur's mouth. He had no idea how he was going to get past them and get out.

All of a sudden Chuggalug was thrown from side to side as the monster seemed to swing round, first one way then the other. The roaring got louder and louder.

Chuggalug crawled slowly up towards the dinosaur's enormous mouth; it was roaring all the time now, and was swinging violently from side to side. He realised that the huge beast was in a fight.

He was nearly at the mouth of the dinosaur and had a horrible thought. What if I get out and find that it's fighting an even bigger dinosaur? He was at the back of the dinosaur's mouth now and could see its great big tonsils dangling at the back of its throat. He swung the piece of bone and stuck it into the side of the dinosaur's throat.

It was only a tiny piece of bone compared to the size of the dinosaur and Chuggalug thought the beast wouldn't even feel it, but suddenly he felt the huge beast draw in its breath. It let out a gigantic cough, and Chuggalug felt himself being carried forward, tumbling over and over, and finally being blown out of the dinosaur's mouth, landing with a thump on the ground.

The dinosaur was very angry now, and Chuggalug looked round to see what it had been fighting. There, behind the back of the great monster was Boing Boing.

As the allosaurus peered down at the ground where Chuggalug lay, Boing Boing sank his teeth into its long tail. The dinosaur twisted round and Boing Boing ran to Chuggalug, who jumped up and onto the tiger's back. He held on tightly as Boing Boing bounded off through the forest, leaving the roaring dinosaur far behind.

Boing Boing ran and ran, and Chuggalug laughed and laughed with relief until they reached the edge of the clearing where Chuggalug lived in a beautiful great tree house his daddy had built high in the branches of a great oak tree.

Chuggalug climbed down from Boing Boing's back and, giving him a big hug, waved goodbye to the big tiger as he ran across the clearing to the oak tree. He climbed up the rope ladder into the tree house and ran to his bedroom.

'Where have you been Chuggalug? Your supper's nearly ready,' his mummy called from the kitchen.

'Just outside playing,' he replied, looking out at Boing Boing disappearing into the forest and thinking that this oak tree, with his tree house in it, was really his favourite tree after all.

The Return of Spring

Chuggalug was looking forward to the time when the snow and rain stopped. That was the time when he would see his best friend, Boing Boing, again.

Every year when the forest became dark and the snow came, Chuggalug's daddy would pull up the rope ladder to the tree house, built high in the branches of the great oak tree in the middle of the clearing in the forest, and they would stay up there, safe above the deep snowdrifts and the floods when the snow turned to rain.

At the same time Boing Boing would disappear. Boing Boing was a very large sabre-toothed tiger who had been Chuggalug's very best friend for ages. Chuggalug knew that Boing Boing disappeared when the snows came and that the great tiger went far away to a place where it did not get so cold as it did in this part of the forest.

He also knew that, in the spring, when the forest came back to life, Boing Boing would return and they would again have many adventures together like always.

At long last the forest was now coming back to life. Chuggalug sat on his bed in the tree house, looking out of the window and across the tree tops to the great dark mountains far away. The sun was shining and the air was filled with the fresh smells of the new forest; the new leaves, the new flowers, and the sounds of the forest animals awakening, the chirping, grunting, and snorting as they searched for food or busied themselves building a den or a nest.

Chuggalug saw something moving below in the clearing. He looked down and saw to his delight, far below, his daddy was standing in the clearing waving to him. Chuggalug whooped with joy, ran out of his bedroom and jumped on to the rope ladder which stretched down all the way to the grassy clearing far below.

'Be careful!' called his mummy, laughing at his eagerness to get down the ladder. 'And don't go off into the forest until your daddy has made sure it's safe.'

'Okay, Mummy, I won't,' Chuggalug called back as he scampered down the rope ladder. He jumped off before he reached the bottom and landed with a thump and a laugh on the soft grass below.

'Steady,' laughed his daddy as he saw Chuggalug land on the grass and run off as fast as he could round the clearing. 'Stay in the clearing until I have a chance to take a look round.'

'Okay,' shouted Chuggalug, just before he tripped, fell and rolled over and over, landing an his back, laughing up at the blue sky and the wonderful bright sunshine.

After a while, his daddy cane back into the clearing. 'It's all right,' he called to Chuggalug, 'There are no dinosaurs to be seen, but don't wander off into the forest.'

'Can I go and look for Boing Boing?' pleaded Chuggalug, who was so looking forward to seeing his friend again, 'Can I please, Daddy?'

'No,' said his daddy. 'Boing Boing will come to see you when he's ready. We have no idea where he'll be at the moment, so just stay in the clearing and play.'

So Chuggalug played in the clearing. He lay down on the grass and rolled down the grassy bank, to the edge of the river which sparkled and gurgled over the stones. He threw stones into the river, and tried to make the flat stones skim over the surface. He played and played all day, stopping every now and then to look round the forest at the edge of the clearing, and listen for any signs of Boing Boing. But Boing Boing still hadn't appeared when he heard his mummy call to him that it was time to come in for bed.

'Oh well,' said his daddy, seeing Chuggalug's sad face and patting him on the head. 'I expect Boing Boing will be here tomorrow, or the next day. But you must remember that he is a wild animal, and you'll just have to be patient until he comes back.'

'I suppose so,' said Chuggalug in a tired voice. 'I just hope he comes back soon.'

But day after day went slowly by, and Boing Boing did not come back.

Chuggalug was very sad. Days had turned into weeks and his friend still hadn't returned. Chuggalug wandered around in the forest, kicking the leaves on the ground, wondering why Boing Boing hadn't come.

Maybe I wasn't a good enough friend, he thought sadly, and Boing Boing has found a new best friend. As more and more days passed he got sadder and sadder and sadder.

One night after Chuggalug had spent ages sitting at his bedroom window looking out over the forest, hoping Boing Boing would appear, his daddy came in and sat down beside him. He explained to Chuggalug that sometimes wild animals got into fights with other animals and could be injured or even killed and that it could be that something had happened to Boing Boing which kept him from coming to see Chuggalug.

'I'm never going to see him again,' said Chuggalug, feeling the tears rise to his eyes. He buried his face in his pillow and eventually fell fast asleep.

When Chuggalug woke up it was still night-time. The house was quiet and he could see the big yellow moon and the stars out of the window. He was wondering what had wakened him when he heard it. Far in the distance a great roar echoed through the forest.

Chuggalug knew that roar. It was Boing Boing.

He jumped out of bed and ran to the rope ladder. He rushed down the ladder and ran off into the forest. He could see by the light of the moon, and just beyond the edge of the clearing there was Boing Boing walking towards him.

Chuggalug ran forward and threw his arms round the great tiger's neck. He hugged him and hugged him, and he could hear the deep purring noise as he buried his face into the warm fur in Boing Boing's chest.

Where have you been?' asked Chuggalug. 'I thought something had happened to you and I would never see you again.'

'Come with me and I'll show you,' said Boing Boing, laughing.

The huge tiger bent down so that Chuggalug could climb on to his back. Boing Boing then bounded off through the trees, into the thickest part of the forest.

They ran and ran until it was getting daylight and Chuggalug could see that they were near the bottom of the great mountains that he had often seen from his bedroom window.

Chuggalug knew that he had never been as far into the forest before, and was still wondering where Boing Boing was taking him when the big sabre-toothed tiger stopped.

Chuggalug climbed down and looked around. 'What is it?' he asked, curiously. 'Why have you brought me all this way?'

Boing Boing gently nudged Chuggalug with his big wet nose, pushing him forward until Chuggalug saw that there was a cave opening in front of him, right at the bottom of the mountain.

Boing Boing nudged him right to the mouth of the cave, and Chuggalug peered in. It was very dark in the cave and at first he could see nothing. Then, as his eyes became accustomed to the dark, Chuggalug saw something move.

He was looking at another huge sabre-toothed tiger, and was just about to turn and run when he was knocked on to his back by first one, then two, then three, then four squealing bundles of fur which landed on his chest.

Chuggalug saw that he had been attacked by four beautiful little sabre-toothed tiger cubs which were now pushing and jostling each other, all trying to lick his face at the same time.

'So this is why you couldn't come earlier,' he laughed to Boing Boing as the small wet tongues tickled his face. 'You had to look after your cubs.'

Chuggalug stood up and saw that the mummy sabre-toothed tiger had come to the mouth of the cave and was lying with her huge furry head resting on her front paws, watching him playing with the cubs.

It was a very happy and tired little boy who eventually untangled himself from the squealing bundle of tiger cubs and climbed on to Boing Boing's back for the journey home.

Back in the tree house, after waving to Boing Boing as he bounded back into the forest, Chuggalug ran to tell his mummy and daddy about the four lovely tiger cubs.

'Well,' said his daddy, 'so that's why Boing Boing didn't come earlier. But you must remember that he might not be able to come here so often if he has cubs to look after.'

But Chuggalug didn't mind. He now knew that Boing Boing was still his friend, and that he would have many games and adventures with the cubs in the days ahead.